Cece
Saves the Planet

Ashley Keller

Illustrated by Jesús Gallardo

ISBN: 978-1-7345680-5-9
Library of Congress Control Number: 2020908285

figfactormedia.com

To my sweet Cece Bee.

You make me want to make the
world a better place.

Come on an adventure with me,
I promise it will be grand.
Let's visit a few of my favorite places,
The ones who save our land.

We need to work together,
It's time to save our planet.
You will learn a few new words as well,
Like sustainable and organic.

Join me at our first stop, to the AQUAPONICS farm we go,
Where fish produce the nutrient to help the lettuce grow.

A giant fish tank, and many long tubes,
They grow all the vegetables in tiny cubes.

Now why is this sustainable, one may ask,
Needing less water and space makes for an easier task.

My next stop is a **BEE FARM**, which gave me such a fright.
The queen bee, the workers. What a beautiful sight.
But don't get me wrong, they have much work to do.
But the way they wiggle and dance, have me wanting to dance, too.

They gather the nectar, bring it back to the hive,
Create delicious honey, and help the queen to survive.

We take that honey, to make medicine or lotion,
Or pour it straight into our tea, what a delightful potion.

How can we help, and make sure to do our part?
Growing a bee-friendly garden would be such a great start!

Ewww, disgusting, what is that smell?

Recycling is something we should all do well.

Here at the RECYCLING PLANT is where our trash becomes treasure,

Making a difference so big, it's hard to measure.

Taking bottles, boxes, or bags,

Making park benches, comic books, or flags,

Go ahead, ask your mom and dad.

If we all recycle, the world will be so glad.

Are those giant swimming pools I see?

Actually, it's a **WATER TREATMENT PLANT**, but just as cool, we guarantee!

When you flush your toilet or run to the sink,

Where does that water go?

What do you think?

It flows right here to get nice and clean,

Then back to our homes,

To be used as drinking water, toilet water, and everything in between.

13

Our next stop is the SOLAR FARM,

And, boy, what a view.

A bunch of beautiful panels,

Shining silver and blue.

When the sun gives off energy,

They catch it so quick.

And save it for later,

Like a sustainable magic trick.

We are here at the **WIND FARM**, and what a great sight,

Windmills moving so fast, they just might take flight.

A slight breeze turns the blades,

Converting it to power.

We save it for later,

To be used at any hour.

I look out my window and what do I see?

A giant green hill and a white floral tree.

Surrounded by buildings, it can get quite sad,

But with this big **GREEN SPACE**, I can't feel bad.

When cars cause pollution and make the air thick,

These wonderful green spaces clean it up quick.

So, whenever you're in the city and need a nice break,

Look for your local green space or river or lake.

While visions of water slides play in my mind,

I'm at the **HYDROPOWER PLANT** to see what I can find.

Flowing water, spinning turbines this place has it all,

They call it a dam, like a giant water wall.

The flow of the water makes the turbines spin,

Which captures energy inside to bring back to the power grid.

HYDROELECTRICITY PLANT

I can't wait for our next stop - do you know
where we are?

You can find them everywhere, you don't have to look far.

A house made of glass, so cozy inside,

A wonderful place for your favorite plants to hide.

No matter the weather, summer, winter, or fall;
inside of a GREENHOUSE it stays warm during all.

Here on the farm I feel one with the land,

Let's visit my favorite farmer to help lend a hand.

Today he told me all about CROP ROTATION,

It's how we plant different items in different formations.

By making the dirt happy and growing more food,

This type of sustainable farming is what we all should do.

How can you help your favorite farmer out?

Remember to buy local, it is better without a doubt.

I love being sustainable, a friend of the land,

And there are so many others who truly understand.

CO-OPS are places where we gather as one,

Helping each other out to get the job done.

Growing food, sharing ideas, or lending a hand,

When you're in a co-op, life can be grand!

Now that you've taken this journey with me,

You can see how sustainable living is the way to be.

Whether you grow a big garden or recycle a letter,

If we all work together, the earth will be better.

FAREWELL!

Glossary of Terms

AQUAPONICS: Aquaponics is the act of growing food by suspending it in water and using fish waste to provide nutrients.

BEEKEEPING: Beekeeping is how keepers maintain hives and collect honey for use in many everyday products.

RECYCLING PLANT: A recycling plant is where abandoned goods go to be reused into different items.

WATER TREATMENT PLANT: A water treatment plant takes soiled or used water and makes it healthy again so that it may be put back into our water systems.

SOLAR ENERGY FIELD: A solar energy field is where panels harvest the sun's power to be put back onto the power grid.

WIND FARM: A wind farm uses windmills in open fields to produce electricity.

GREENSPACE: A green space is a park or area of grass in an urban environment, such as New York City.

HYDROPOWER PLANT: In Hydropower plants, by harnessing the power of fast moving water, a generator can convert it into usable energy.

GREENHOUSE: A greenhouse is a structure made from transparent material that allows sun rays to get to the plants, but keeps heat inside of the house.

CROP ROTATION: Crop Rotation is a process used by farmers by growing specific plants in certain regions to prevent pests and weeds, and help with nutrient control.

CO-OP: A co-op is a group of individuals all with the same goals for economic and sustainability practices.

About the Author:

Ashley Keller started her sustainable journey in 2017 with backyard beekeeping. In 2018, she opened one of the first aquaponic lettuce farms in the Midwest, with her brother. She believes that the first step in making the planet a better place is educating future generations.

Visit **ceceshoneybees.com** and **fishygreenorganic.com** for more sustainable ideas!

Made in the USA
Coppell, TX
29 November 2020

42440118R00021